You may have heard of ships.

They float on water and carry people and things.

DISCARD

You may have heard of the sea.
It's when water gets together with a plan to surround us.

You may have heard of night.

It's what happens when the earth turns away from the sun.

And last, you may have heard of beauty

It's what we call something that pleases the eye so much we ache and say *Oh!*

But did you realize that of all the world's most beautiful sights, there is nothing more beautiful than a ship and its lights on the sea at night?

This is true. This is a factual book.

Look at this ship. It is a container ship, full of giant boxes of things. On this ship there are giant boxes of toys, and giant boxes of bicycles, and giant boxes of oven mitts and basketballs. And this ship is lighted by a thousand lights, and these lights are reflected on the to-and-fro obsidian sea. Has there ever been anything more beautiful?

No!

Maybe there is! Maybe it's this! This is a trawler, a kind of fishing ship. Look at its strange arms. Look at its strange face. Look at its lights as they are doubled on the water. Has there been a prettier picture? We say no!

Actually, maybe this is better. This is a RoRo. Is there anything better than the name RoRo? Yes, there is something better, and that is the sight of the RoRo moving swiftly through the water at night. RoRos are so named because they carry cars! They roll on, and roll off. Thus, RoRo! Which makes them the best-ever of all boats.

But no! There is this! This is an exploration vessel.
It's designed to explore the unknown oceans! To map
the sea floor! To find new underwater species!

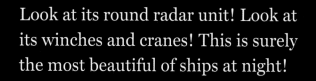

Look at its round radar unit! Look at its winches and cranes! This is surely the most beautiful of ships at night!

Oh wait. Look here. This is a bulker. See it, so long and so low. It's built to carry corn and cement and heavy stuff like that. Bulkers are everywhere!

And they sail at night, and with their
lights on they go from boring bulkers
to something magical and triumphant.
Look! How can you disagree?

Forget what we said about all other ships being the most beautiful. This is a paddlewheel ferryboat, and nothing ever has more gorgeously floated in the night. Look at the lights! So many lights!

Ferryboats like this were developed on the great Mississippi River, and are known for chugging up and down rivers, with giant paddlewheels spinning in the back, to carry forth all the passengers.

Never could there be anything prettier.

Except these! These galleons! Have you heard of a galleon? Not a gallon—a galleon! They were great and fast sail-driven boats favored by European sailors and even pirates back in the day, and were once lighted with oil-powered lanterns. Now, the antique galleons that still sail the sea are decorated with modern lights inside and out, up and down, and when they appear at night, like illuminated dreams of the past, they are the best of all things on water.

But perhaps you like ice! Perhaps you like ships that blast through ice with lights of every color! Do you? Do you? It could be that you do. This is an icebreaker, an indestructible and brave ship that cuts through ice near the Earth's poles, forging a path for other ships. With its purpose and its lights that turn and sweep, surely the icebreaker is the most stunning of ocean vessels.

Or! Or! Or! It could be these. These are known as junks. They come from China, and have been around for a thousand years or more. Look at their beautiful sails, which look like the wings of dragons! Junks are used to move cargo and people and are still used today, all over the waterways of Asia—from India to the Philippines. There can be nothing better to look at ever on water.

Unless you come across this! This is a small fishing boat, a kind often seen all over the world, from Taiwan to the Mediterraean Sea. A few people will operate the boat, and they will fish at night, using bright lights to bring the fish to the surface. Why? Because fish are drawn to the moon! This is true.

When the moon is bright, tiny animals called plankton come to the surface, and then tiny fish come to eat the plankton, and bigger fish come to eat the smaller fish. So these fisherpeople will use bright lights to mimic the moon to fish for fish!

But maybe you don't like fish. The smell? The scales? Maybe, instead, you like Paris. This is a river boat designed to cruise up and down the Seine, the river that winds through Paris, France. See how low it is, how sleek? It needs to be, to fit under the low bridges that are everywhere in Paris and allow people and cars and bikes to cross the river.

And when they cross the river, at night, they see—and someday you will see!—these low river boats shushing, shushing through the golden Parisian water. You could travel the world and find nothing anywhere more beautiful, period.

But maybe you're tired. We have seen so many boats, from all over the globe, and maybe you are ready to rest. If you are ready to rest, there is no better place than on a houseboat. A houseboat is exactly what it sounds like—a house that is also a boat.

A floating home! And when a floating home has dimmed its lights, when everyone inside is ready to sleep, there is nothing prettier, nothing happier, nothing better anywhere on the sea.